TO
MATILDA

First published in hardback in Great Britain by Digital Leaf in 2013

ISBN: 978-1-909428-02-7

Text copyright © James Thorp 2013. Illustrations copyright © Angus Mackinnon 2013
The author and illustrator assert the moral right to be identified as the author and illustrator of the work.

digitalleaf

The WEASEL PUFFIN UNICORN BABOON PIG LOBSTER Race

~ BY JAMES THORP AND ANGUS MACKINNON ~

The weasel
puffin, unicorn
baboon, pig
lobster race

began
one pinky morning
as the sun
climbed into space.

With creatures from around the world,
the thinnest to the thickest,
all gathered round the starting line,
to see which one was quickest.

From six to one
they counted down
invited by
the queen,

to bang their rowdy
pots and pans
and set the racers
fleeing.

'Welcome to my garden,'
sang the unicorn with pride,
as they leapt into the forest
leaving lobster far behind.

The path was overcrowded
with a scribble-bed of weed,
so lobster and his giant claw
was snailish in his speed.

'I'll win this barmy race,' he thought,
'and beat those other beasts,
but first of all I think I'll need
a sneaky way to cheat.'

So joining all the berries
using scrambled egg for glue,
he sailed off down the river
on a raspberry canoe.

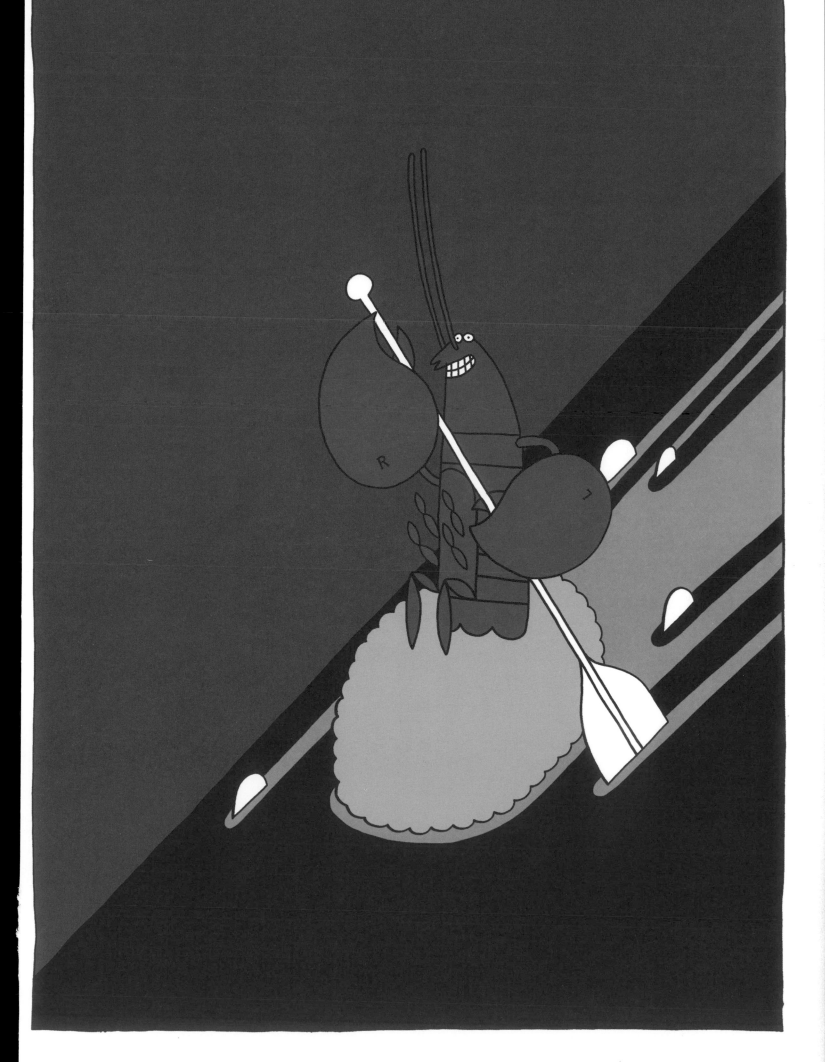

'Now welcome to my bathtub,'
sang the lobster with a smile,
as they raced into the ocean
leaving pig behind by miles.

The sea was cold and slimy
with a shoal of fishes grim,
so even with his goggles on
the pig was scared to swim.

'I'll win this queasy race,' he thought,
'and beat those other beasts,
but first of all I think I'll need
a sneaky way to cheat.'

Just then he smelled a funny shape
come bubbling through the green,
and what should take him on his way
but a chocolate submarine.

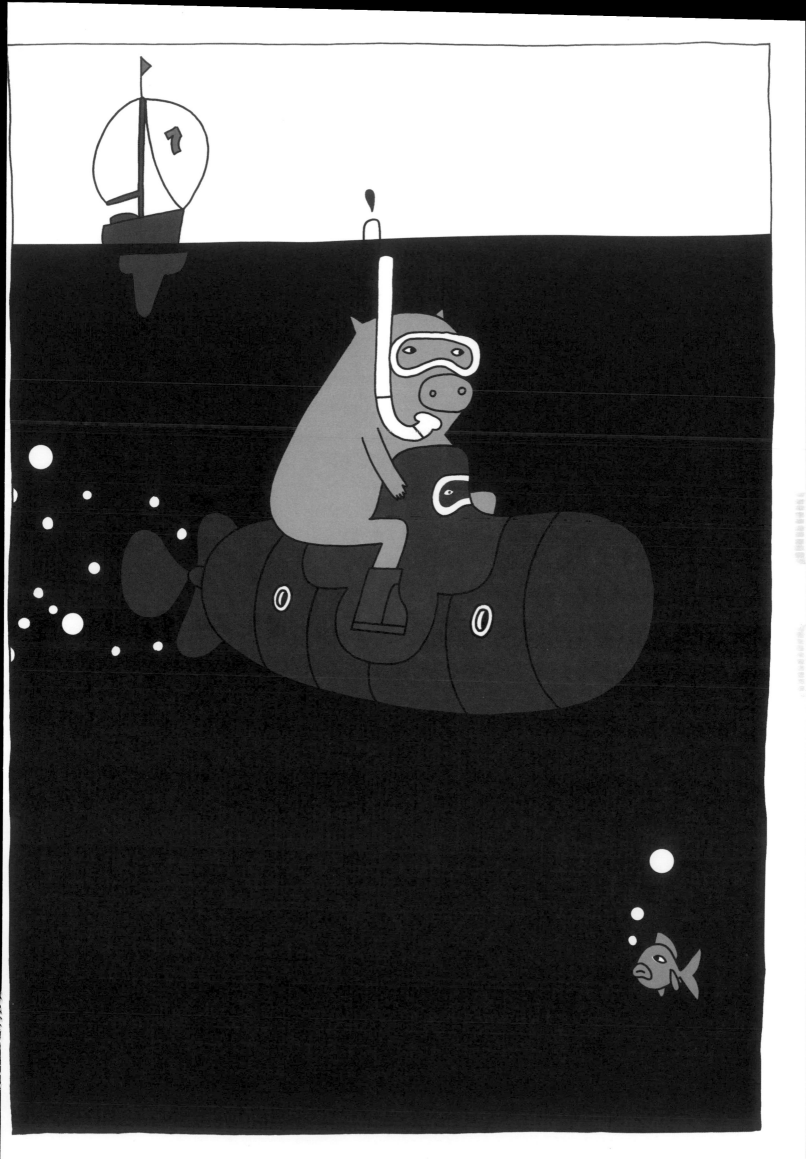

'Say, welcome to my mudworld,'
sang the pig to old baboon,
as they left him with his trumpet
in the gurgling swamps of goo.

The path was slick and soggy
like a double-soup of sludge,
so the more he tried to move his arms
the more he couldn't budge.

'I'll win this mucky race,' he thought,
    'and beat those other beasts,
    but first of all I think I'll need
        a sneaky way to cheat.'

Just then a rope came tumbling down
    from high above baboon
and there to drag him from the swamp
        - a coconut balloon.

'Now welcome to my playground,'
sang baboon with quite a laugh,
as they raced into the jungle
leaving puffin out of puff.

The track was thorny zigzags
and a tangle-web of hands,
so every time he turned a zig
he'd zag his underpants.

'I'll win this snaggy race,' he thought,
'and beat those other beasts,
but first of all I'm going to need
a sneaky way to cheat.'

Just then he stumbled on a thing
like finding gold, but bigger,
and soon was drilling underground
on a big banana digger.

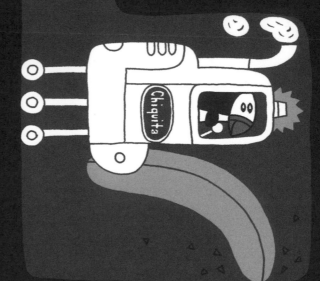

'Ha ha, ha ha, ha ha ha,'
sang puffin from the lead,
as they clambered up the rock face
leaving weasel wobbly-kneed.

The path was steep as noses,
it had bubble-holes of drool,
so every inch the weasel climbed
he'd fall back down by two. 'I'll...

'...win this slippy race,' he thought,
'and beat those other beasts,
but first of all I'm going to need
a sneaky way to cheat.'

So bounding up and down the shore
to see what could be seen,
he took a leap and jumped the cliff
from a custard trampoline.

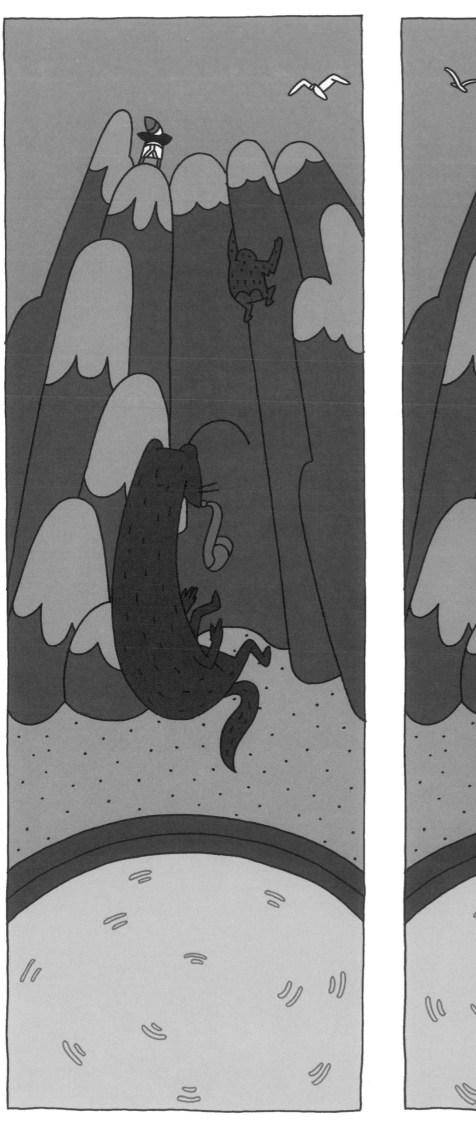

'Ah, welcome to my lovely home,'
said weasel with a whistle,
as unicorn began to cry
from eating too much thistle.

The others through the orchard ran
all hoping they could win,
as unicorn, with belly ache,
drib-dribbled down his chin.

'I'll never win this race,' he cried,
'and beat those other beasts,
but better lose it, fair and square,
than beat them as a cheat.'

So sighing in his pool of tears,
a loser not a winner,
he plodded up the grassy path
to finish off his dinner...

The weasel
puffin, unicorn
baboon, pig
lobster race

was finished
in a mess of legs
and blur
of silly face.

Said all the crowd
that saw them pass,
'It's surely
a dead heat',

but for a snail
who on the trail
had plainly
seen them cheat.

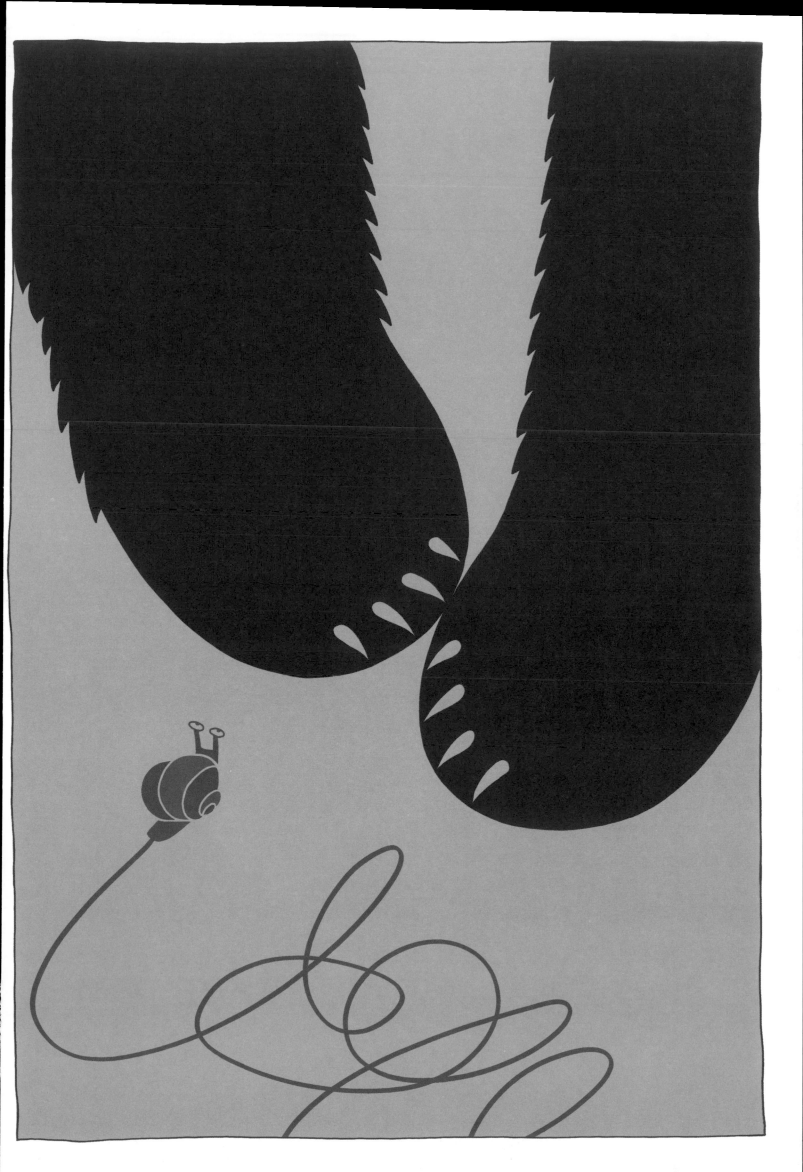

'In big banana diggers
and a coconut balloon,' he said
(speaking from the apple tree
beside the garden shed),

'they flew on custard trampolines
and floated down the ooze,
on smelly chocolate submarines
and raspberry canoes'.

So limping through the finish line
to cheers of 'run run run,'
the unicorn, to his surprise,
was told that he had won.

The creatures from around the world
put down their pots and pans
and crowded round the unicorn
to stroke him with their hands.

They stroked him on his fluffy chin
and stroked him on his head,
then turning round to say goodnight...

...they all went home to bed.

CHEATS FOOL

Serves 2

INGREDIENTS

12 RASPBERRIES
1 BANANA SKIN REMOVED
200g CUSTARD
50g CHOCOLATE BITS (SMASHED IN A BAG)
1 TABLESPOON COCONUT FLAKES

PREPARATION

1. WASH HANDS
2. GET BREAKFAST BOWL
3. ADD INGREDIENTS TO BOWL
4. EAT WITH A SPOON

CHEATS FOOL

Serves 2

INGREDIENTS

12 RASPBERRIES
1 BANANA SKIN REMOVED
200g CUSTARD
50g CHOCOLATE BITS (SMASHED IN A BAG)
1 TABLESPOON COCONUT FLAKES

PREPARATION

1. WASH HANDS
2. GET BREAKFAST BOWL
3. ADD INGREDIENTS TO BOWL
4. EAT WITH A SPOON